AF575493

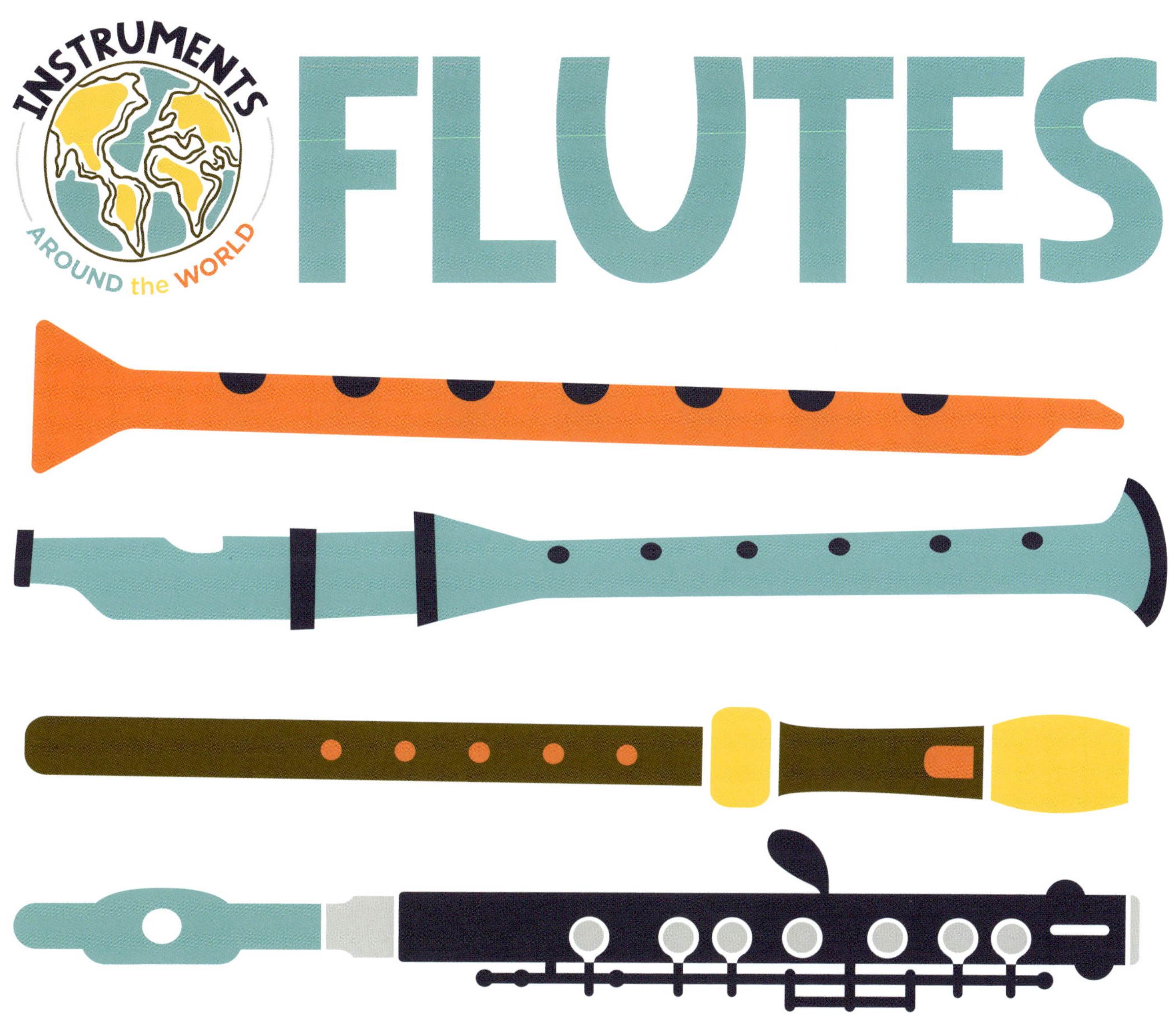

Roberta Baxter

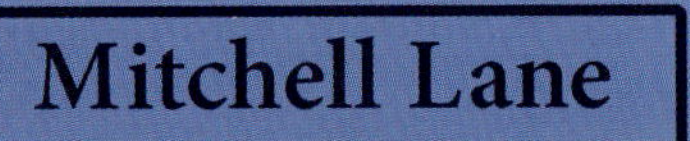

2001 SW 31st Avenue
Hallandale, FL 33009
www.mitchelllane.com

First Edition, 2021.

Author: Roberta Baxter
Designer: Ed Morgan
Editor: Sharon F. Doorasamy

Little Mitchie is an imprint of Mitchell Lane Publishers.

Title: Musical Instruments Around the World: Flutes / by Roberta Baxter
Description: Hallandale, FL :
Mitchell Lane Publishers, [2021]

Series: Instruments Around the World
Library bound ISBN: 978-1-68020-592-3
eBook ISBN: 978-1-68020-593-0

Photo credits: pps. 4-5 Spencer Imbrock on Unsplash, pp. 6-7 Jyotirmoy Gupta on Unsplash, p. 8-9 freepik.com, p. 10-11 David South / Alamy Stock Photo, p. 12 Patrick Brinksman on Unsplash, pp. 14-15, Shutterstock.com, pp. 16-17 E&E Image Library Heritage Images/Newscom, pp. 18-19 NASA Image Collection / Alamy Stock Photo, p. 20-21 freepik.com, p. 22 Michael DeFreitas / DanitaDelimont.com Danita Delimont Photography/Newscom

CONTENTS

Words in **bold** can be found in the Glossary.

People everywhere love music. Sometimes the music is singing. Other times, people play **instruments**.

A flute is an instrument in the shape of a tube. A person who plays the flute is called a flute player or a flutist. They are also called flautists. Flutes reach high notes when played.

GERMANY

Flutes go way back in history. The earliest flutes were made of bone. **Archaeologists** found a flute in a cave in Germany. It is more than 40,000 years old and made of ivory. The ivory came from a **mammoth tusk**. Today, flutes played in concerts are made of metal.

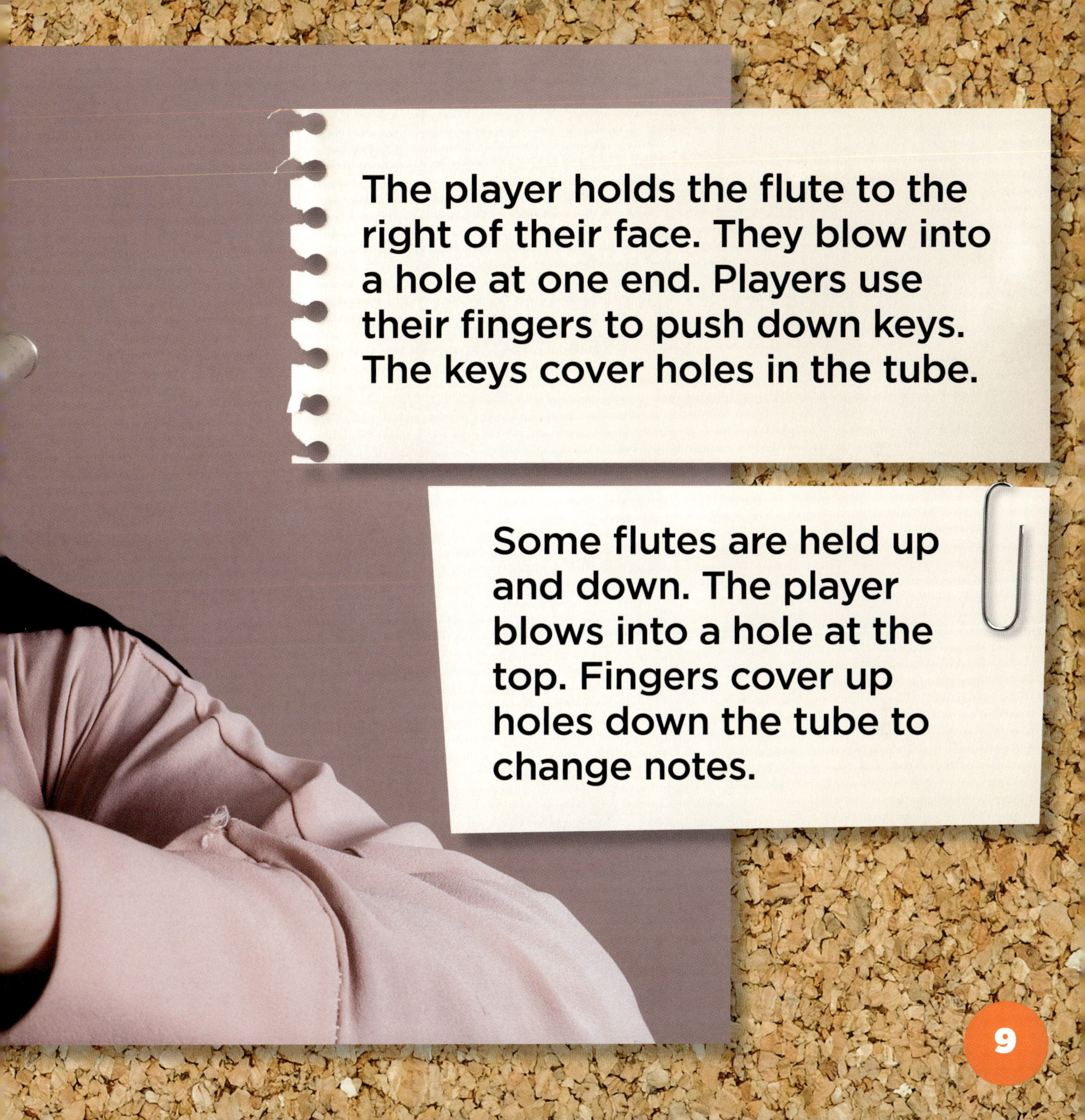

The player holds the flute to the right of their face. They blow into a hole at one end. Players use their fingers to push down keys. The keys cover holes in the tube.

Some flutes are held up and down. The player blows into a hole at the top. Fingers cover up holes down the tube to change notes.

People play different kinds of flutes. The *dizi* is a flute from China. This flute is played sideways. It is played in Chinese folk songs and **operas**. It is made of **bamboo**.

Nose flutes are played in the Philippines. They are played in New Zealand, Myanmar, and Hawaii too. They are played with air blown out of a nostril.

MYANMAR
HAWAII
PHILIPPINES
NEW ZEALAND

In India, musicians play the *bansuri*. It is a sideways flute made of bamboo. It is larger than the metal flutes played in the United States.

Madagascar is an island off of Africa. The flute there is called a *sodina*. It is played up and down. It is smaller than most flutes.

The *shakuhachi* is a Japanese bamboo flute. It is played by blowing across one end of a bamboo tube. It is held up and down. It has five finger holes.

妙音
妙音
暗

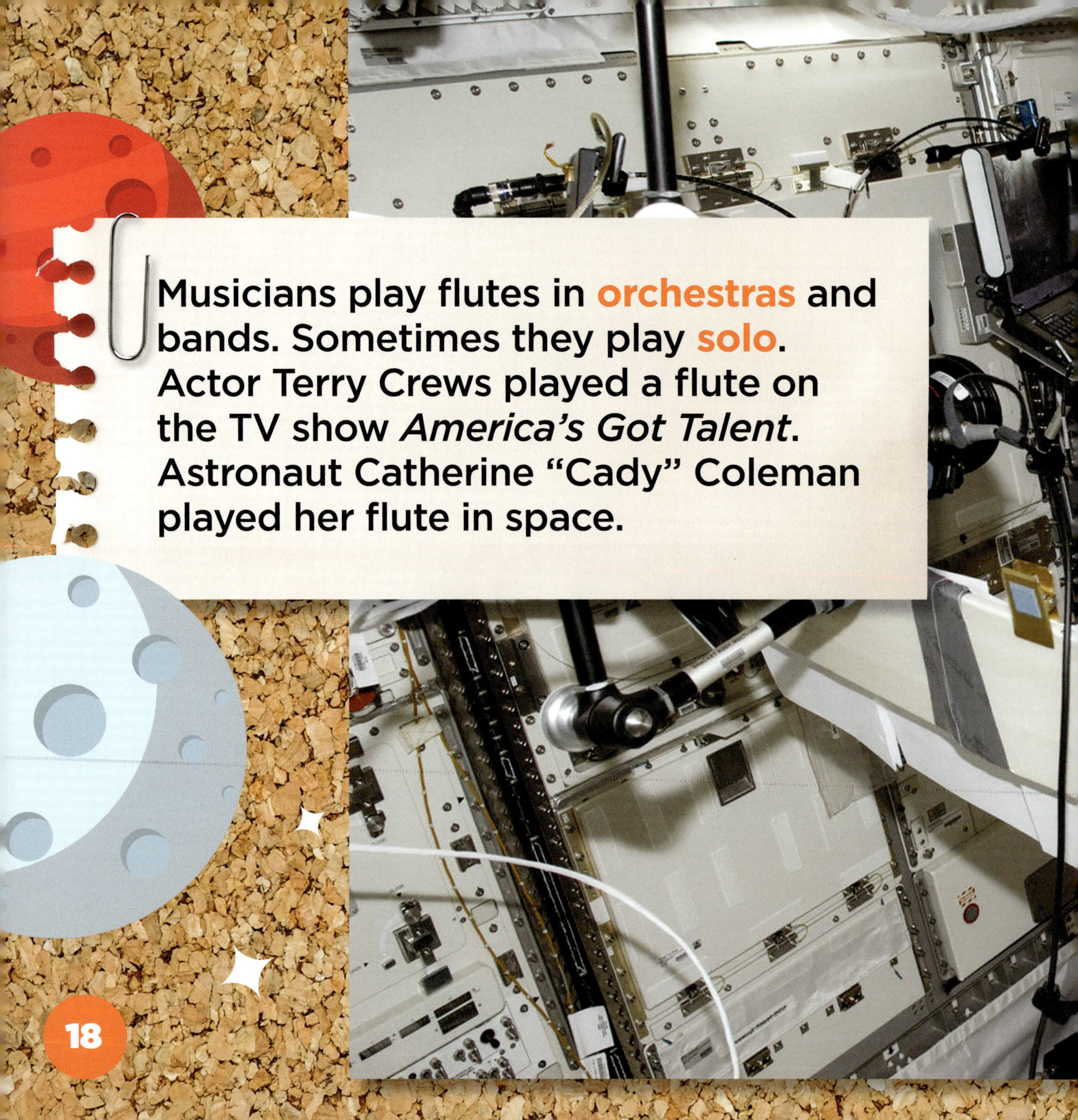

Musicians play flutes in **orchestras** and bands. Sometimes they play **solo**. Actor Terry Crews played a flute on the TV show *America's Got Talent*. Astronaut Catherine "Cady" Coleman played her flute in space.

The flute is a favorite instrument. You will find it played in Africa and Asia. You'll hear it in music in Europe, Australia, or the Americas.

Want to hear the flute? Go to a concert. Listen to CDs. Even better, learn to play it yourself!

MAKE YOUR OWN ZAMPOÑA

The *zampoña* is a type of pan flute, or panpipe, found in Peru in South America. You can make one. You will need five drinking straws, scissors, a ruler, and tape. If your straws have flexible tips, cut off the tips.

1. Use your ruler to measure and cut four straws into different lengths. Cut an inch off of one straw. Cut two inches off of a second straw. Three inches off of a third. Four inches off of a fourth.
2. Line up your five straws from longest to shortest.
3. Lay down a piece of tape with the sticky side facing up. Place the longest straw on the tape first, near the left edge. Place the remaining straws on the tape. Keep the top edge of the straws as straight as possible.
4. Once the straws are placed, wrap the ends of the tape up and around the other side of the straws until the ends meet.
5. Hold the panpipe below your lips, with the uneven ends pointing down. Blow across the tops of the straws like you're blowing across the top of a pop bottle. A long straw produces a deep or low sound. A short straw produces a high note.

If at first your flute sounds a little flat, don't get discouraged. Practice makes perfect!

WHERE TO FIND FREE, USED, OR INEXPENSIVE INSTRUMENTS

- **Ask your teacher.**
- **Talk to your grandparents.** They might have some in their homes.
- **Ask the music director** at your **church**, **synagogue**, **temple**, or **mosque**.
- **Go with your parents** to **yard sales**, **flea markets**, and **secondhand shops**.
- **Ask your parents** to check **Internet websites** for discounted instruments.
- **Contact your local symphony** or a **local charity** that supports music programs.

GLOSSARY

archaeologist
Someone who studies old cultures and objects

bamboo
A plant that has strong hollow stems

instrument
An object that makes music when played by a person

mammoth
A very large, woolly animal that no longer exists; mammoths were bigger than elephants

opera
A story set to music

orchestra
A group of musicians who play different kinds of instruments together

solo
Done by one person

tusk
Pointed teeth that come out of the mouth of some animals

FURTHER READING

Barton, Chris. *88 Instruments*. Knopf books for Young Readers, 2016.

Landau, Elaine. *Is the Flute for You?* Lerner Publications, 2013.

Levin, Robert. *A Child's Introduction to the Orchestra*. Black Dog & Leventhal, 2019.

Rau, Dana Meachen. *Making Musical Instruments*. Cherry Lake Publishing, 2016.

INDEX

ABOUT THE AUTHOR

ROBERTA BAXTER began playing the flute in the 6th grade. She still enjoys flute and band music today. Roberta is the author of more than 45 nonfiction books for children of all ages. She lives in Colorado.